This book belongs to:

GRACIE GOAT'S
BIG BIKE RACE

Story by Erin Mirabella

Illustrations by Lisa Horstman

VELOpress

Boulder, Colorado

Gracie Goat was playing with her friends in the park.

"Guess what?"

Howard Horse announced. "I'm going to be in a bike race. My cousin Helen rides for a professional cycling team. She is racing at the Summer Corn Festival, and she said there is a race for kids, too. I get to wear her team jersey."

Everyone thought Howard was lucky. They wanted to be in the bike race, too.

Howard liked that idea. "We can be a cycling team," he said.

Everyone got really excited—everyone except Gracie. She wanted to disappear. These were Gracie's best friends, but they didn't know her big secret.

Gracie did not know how to ride a bike.

"Can we all borrow jerseys?"
Chelsea Chicken asked.

"I hope so. Then we would look like a real
cycling team," said Howard.

"I could beat your cousin," said Shawn Sheep.

"No way," said Howard. "She's fast. She has
won races all over the world."

"I could still beat her," said Shawn. He
blushed when everyone laughed.

Gracie didn't laugh. She was too upset. If she did not learn how to ride her bike, she would be the only one not on the team. She really wanted to be on the team!

She watched a little worm squirm into a hole in the ground. She wished she could crawl into the hole, too.

"Hey, spacey Gracie," said Howard, waving his hoof in front of her face. "Yes or no?" he asked.

Gracie had not heard the question. "Yes," she said quickly.

"Great," said Howard. "I'll ask Helen if we can borrow seven jerseys for the race."

Gracie gulped.

What had she done?

She'd just signed up for a bike race
and she couldn't even ride a bike yet.
She started to walk home.

Gracie walked in her front door and burst into tears.
She head-butted the couch.

Grandma Goat rushed in to see what was wrong.

Between sobs, Gracie told Grandma everything.

Grandma hugged Gracie. "The race is not for a few weeks," she said. "That should be plenty of time to learn to ride your bike."

"But Grandma, I'm too scared to learn," whispered Gracie.

Grandma gently rocked Gracie, and asked why she was scared to ride her bike.

"I might fall off and get hurt," said Gracie. "But I really want to ride with my friends."

"Then that settles it. Let's go practice," said Grandma.

"No, wait! I can't," said Gracie. "What if a tree branch falls on my head?

"What if I crash into Miss Ruby Rabbit's vegetable garden and beet juice stains me red forever? That would be awful."

Grandma laughed and said, "Gracie, you're goofy. What's really bothering you?"

Gracie sighed. "I'm afraid I won't be able to learn," she admitted.

"What is the worst thing that could happen if you *do* try and don't learn to ride your bike?" asked Grandma.

"My friends might laugh at me and I won't be able to race on the cycling team," said Gracie.

"OK, and what is the worst thing that will happen if you *do not* try to learn to ride your bike?" asked Grandma.

"My friends might laugh at me and I won't be able to race on the cycling team," repeated Gracie.

"Right. So what do you have to lose by trying?" asked Grandma.

"Nothing, I guess. But what if I can't do it?" asked Gracie.

"Everyone fails sometimes," said Grandma. "When you fail, you try again, and you get better."

Gracie thought about this. She decided Grandma was really smart!

Our First Baby, Gwen

Climbing Mt. Kilimanjaro

Whee!

First Solo Flight

edding

Gwen—

Gracie picked up Grandma's photo album. She admired the pictures of Grandma flying a plane and climbing a mountain. "I bet you are not scared of anything." Gracie said.

Grandma smiled shyly and whispered, "I am scared of something."

"What?" Gracie whispered back, leaning in real close.

"I'm scared to get my ears pierced," said Grandma.

Gracie could not believe it. "I can't wait to get my ears pierced for my birthday."

"I wish I was brave like you," Grandma said.

Gracie shook her head and said, "I'm not brave. I'm scared to ride my bike, remember?"

"I'll make you a deal," said Grandma, with a sparkle in her eyes. "If you learn to ride your bike, then I'll get my ears pierced with you."

"It's a deal," said Gracie.

Outside, Gracie sat on her bike, while Grandma held on to the back. Gracie took a deep breath and started to pedal. Grandma let go.

Gracie had barely started moving when she crashed right into a bush. "Oops," she said.

Over and over again she tried to ride, but every time Grandma let go, she fell. Each time Gracie fell, she got back up and tried again. She tried to learn from her mistakes, but it wasn't easy. She made a lot of mistakes.

Finally, after all her practice, it happened. When Grandma let go, Gracie didn't look back, and she kept on riding. She started to wobble, first to the right, then to the left, but she kept on pedaling and didn't fall over. She was riding all by herself.

"Grandma, look! I'm riding my bike!"

yelled Gracie. "Wow, I did it!" She was even brave enough to reach out and ring her bell.

Gracie practiced every day for the race. She loved riding with her friends.

She rode to the park with Chelsea,

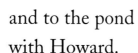

to Bert's Bike Shop with Shawn,

and to the pond with Howard.

She couldn't wait to race at the Summer Corn Festival with her friends.

On race day, Howard's dad loaded all of the bikes onto his car and drove the kids to the race. Gracie thought the car looked funny with all of their bikes on top.

The race was downtown. The streets were blocked off for the race, and professional cyclists had come from all over to compete. Lots of other kids had come to race, too.

Helen Horse rode up to Howard and his friends while they were getting their bikes ready.

The first thing Shawn noticed was her strong legs. "Maybe I couldn't beat you in a race," he said.

"I told you so," said Howard. Everyone laughed.

Gracie loved Helen's jersey. It had a big "K" on the front, for Helen's team, the Kalamazoo Flyers. She asked if they got to wear the same kind.

"You sure do," said Helen, and handed a jersey to each of them.

Chelsea Chicken shrieked with delight.

"Why are there pockets in the back of the jersey?" Peter Pig asked.

"We keep things we need for the race in the pockets, like snacks and a rain jacket," said Helen.

"I'm going to put pizza in mine," Peter said.

Helen laughed. "Pizza is too messy," she said.

"Not for me!" said Peter.

Soon it was race time. Gracie and her friends lined up on the start line. They were excited because they looked like a real cycling team in their jerseys. Gracie snugged up her helmet and gripped her handlebars tightly.

The starting whistle blew, and they were off.
Gracie pumped her legs as hard as she could. She
could not believe she was riding in a bike race.

Gracie was behind Howard and Dana Duck when Howard suddenly hit a pothole in the road. His water bottle flew out of its holder and landed in the street.

Dana swerved to miss it.

Dougie Dog ran over the bottle and smashed it flat as a pancake.

"Yikes," yelped Dougie.

Gracie thought Howard could win the race. She was worried that having no water would hurt his chances. She sprinted up to him, and gave him her water bottle.

"Here," she gasped. "Take mine."

Howard said, "Thanks,"
and took a big gulp of water.

They raced down the street, and as they rounded the corner Gracie could see the finish line. Helen and her friends lined the course, cheering them on.

"This is so much fun," thought Gracie. "I love this!"

Then she heard Grandma yell,

"Go, Gracie, go!"

Gracie rode as hard as she could.

She went so fast she thought her wheels would catch on fire.

All too soon the race was over.

Gracie didn't win. She finished in tenth place, but she had a great time and couldn't stop smiling.

Howard won the race. Gracie was proud.

Howard's dad took the team out for pizza to celebrate their win.

A few weeks later, Grandma and Gracie sat in the earring shop.

"Happy Birthday," said Grandma.

"Thanks, Grandma. Are your ear lobes ready?" Gracie asked.

"I guess. I'm scared it will hurt," Grandma said.

"It might, but think about how pretty you will look," Gracie said.

She held Grandma's hoof. Grandma Goat squeezed back so hard that Gracie thought her hoof would break.

Grandma and Gracie left the shop feeling proud of their new red earrings.

All About Cycling

A person who rides a bike is called a cyclist. Most cyclists ride for fun with their friends. Some cyclists are competitive cyclists and race their bikes. The best racing cyclists in the world compete in the Summer Olympic Games.
There are different kinds of bikes and places to ride them:

there is road cycling, which is done on the streets;

track cycling, which is done on a special track called a velodrome;

mountain biking,
which is done on dirt
and rock trails;

and BMX cycling,
which is done over dirt jumps.

Fitness Fact

Helen Horse told the team that drinking water
during exercise helps the body work well.
She said they might not be able to ride
as fast if they didn't drink enough water.
Cyclists have to work hard in a race, and as they
sweat they lose water from their bodies.
Drinking water puts it back.

Gracie laughed when Helen told them
how to know whether they had enough water
in their bodies. She said you should look at the
color of your pee. If your pee is light yellow,
then your body has enough water. If your pee is
dark yellow, you need to drink more water. Helen
said it was funny, but true.

For Grandma Helen
Your courage, optimism, and love of reading inspire me.

Gracie Goat's Big Bike Race
Text copyright © 2007 by Erin Mirabella
Illustrations copyright © 2007 by Lisa Horstman

For information on purchasing VeloPress books,
call 800/234-8356 or visit www.velopress.com.

07 08 09 / 10 9 8 7 6 5 4 3 2 1

VeloPress
1830 North 55th Street
Boulder, Colorado 80301-2700 USA
303/440-0601
Fax 303/444-6788
E-mail velopress@insideinc.com

First Edition

Design by Debbie Berne,
Herter Studio LLC, San Francisco

Distributed in the United States and Canada by
Publishers Group West

Library of Congress Cataloging-in-Publication Data

Mirabella, Erin.
  Gracie goat's big bike race / story by Erin Mirabell[
  illustrations by Lisa Horstman.
    p. cm.
  ISBN-13: 978-1-931382-88-5
  (hard cover : alk. paper)
  ISBN-10: 1-931382-88-3
  1. Cycling—Juvenile literature. I. Horstman, Lisa
  ill. II. Title.
GV1043.5.M57 2007
796.6—dc22

2006022181